The CODE BREAKER

SALLY PIERSON DILLON

REVIEW AND HERALD® PUBLISHING ASSOCIATION
HAGERSTOWN, MD 21740

The author assumes full responsibility for the accuracy
of all facts and quotations as cited in this book.

Scripture quotations marked Message are from *The
Message.* Copyright © 1993. Used by permission of
NavPress Publishing Group.

This book was
Edited by Richard W. Coffen
Designed by Robert J. Ritzenthaler, Jr.
Cover illustration by Scott Snow
Typeset: 11/13 Optima

PRINTED IN U.S.A.

99 98 97 96 95   5 4 3 2 1

R&H Cataloging Service
Dillon, Sally Pierson, 1959-
    The Code Breaker

    I. Title.

                813.54

ISBN 0-8280-0981-3

Conte

NOISE IN THE RADIATOR

"I hate it here; I just hate it. I wish we'd never moved," complained Donnie.

"I know, honey," said Mom, smoothing his hair back and propping his cast up on a pillow. "This has been a hard week for you."

"I had to go to a new school. I don't know anybody. I don't have any friends. And now I have a broken leg and have to stay in bed for two weeks."

"Well, you wouldn't have broken your leg if you weren't showing off to those girls," said Michael from the safety of the doorway.

"You're not helping things," said Mom. "Please go downstairs."

"OK." Michael grinned wickedly as he disappeared.

"I wish we had never come here to take care of Dad's nasty old grandma."

"Grandma Kirkie isn't nasty. She's old and she's sick, and we've come here to take care of her for a little while until the family decides what to do. She really can't take care of herself since she had that stroke."

"Boy, I'll say. All she does is sit there and drool."

"You need to be kind. All you do is sit here and complain, and we still love you. Why don't you try to get some rest. I'm going downstairs and sit Grandma up for a little while and feed her some lunch. I'll come back and check on you in a little while. Would you like me to move the TV in here?"

"What good would *that* do?" asked Donnie. "I'm too old for *Sesame Street* and Mister Rogers, and the only stuff on during the day are the soaps and Donahue's weirdo of the day."

"Fine. Count the cracks in the plaster then. I'll be back to check on you in about an hour," Mom said as she disappeared from the doorway.

Donnie's frown deepened. He glared at the neon green cast that encased his leg from his foot up to the top of his thigh. *The days of plain white casts are over*, he thought to himself, remembering the brightly colored rolls of fiberglass wrap he was allowed to choose from. He scowled. It didn't matter how cool the colors were, he hated the cast. He hated everything about having a broken leg; like how much it hurt just to barely move, or when anyone bumped the bed or walked too hard on the floor, or like how he wouldn't be able to bear any weight on it for 10 days, and how hard it was to get to the bathroom without walking. Mom had brought him a strange-looking jug from the hospital to help with that. Donnie reddened with embarrassment, remembering his teacher's visit. She had brought him some flowers in green florist paper.

"Here," she said. "I'll just put them here in this, er, vase." He was mortified! He frowned at the notebook with her note in it. It read:

Dear Donnie,

I was so sorry to hear about your leg. While you are home recovering, you may work on a writing project for lan-

guage credit so that you don't get too far behind.

1. Draw your family tree. Start with yourself and work backward, or start with a person in your family and work forward, but it must include you.

2. Write a short story about each person in the tree.

3. Number the spots on the tree to match the stories.

Good luck and hope to see you back in school soon!

Sincerely,
Mrs. Brown

Donnie put the letter down and started leafing through the magazine that his brother, Michael, had brought for him. He flipped from page to page aimlessly, not even concentrating on his favorite section.

I guess I could write about how Mom went to Africa when she was a little girl, he thought. *Her family were the last missionaries to go over by boat. Or I could write about how Grandma Kirkie got her name. That's pretty funny.*

Grandma Jo had told the story so many times that Donnie knew it by heart. Back when Dad was only 3 years old, Grandma Kirkie had gotten her first permanent. Before that she had long straight hair. She had come home from the hairdresser's with a short hair cut and her hair was very fuzzy. The perm had made her hair too curly, and she hated it. Her husband (a Grandpa Donnie had never met because he had died before Donnie was born) teased her unmercifully, calling her "Curly."

Dad, with the usual sensitivity of a 3-year-old, tried to call her "Curly" too, only he had a little trouble getting his speech going in the right direction and ended up calling her "Kirkie" instead. It stuck. Everyone in the whole family called her Kirkie from then on! It struck Donnie that he didn't even know what Grandma Kirkie's real name was.

One thing was for sure, Donnie couldn't imagine Grandma Kirkie without curly hair. She wore her curly wig day and night and got really upset if it ever came off, even to be washed!

He had seen her without it only once. She was bald as an egg except for a few long white strands of hair. Mom had taken off Grandma Kirkie's wig to wash and dry her head, and she was fumbling around angrily trying to find it and put it back on.

I guess she got used to being "Curly" after all, he thought.

Suddenly, he became aware of a tapping noise coming from the radiator. Tap, tap, tap. Bang, bang, bang. Tap, tap, tap. "I hate this old house," he grumbled to himself. "It's full of creaks and noises. Even the radiators make noise. You'd think that in a fancy old house like this they could've put in a modern heating system. It's amazing that these big old water radiators even work." The tapping continued.

Michael appeared in the doorway, cautiously. "You need anything, Donnie?"

"No. But that dumb radiator sure is making a lot of noise. Listen."

"Wow," Michael said, "it almost sounds like a code. Three short taps, three long taps, and three short taps. Isn't that SOS in Morse code?"

Is It a Ghost?

"I don't know," said Donnie. "I don't know Morse code."

"I don't either," said Michael. "I just saw it on movie when a ship was in trouble. It sounds like what they were doing with their old telegraph machine. Do you suppose the radiator's in trouble?"

"Don't be stupid," said Donnie.

"Yeah, well," said Michael grinning, "that is kind of stupid. But as old as this house is, you never know."

If any house on that block ever looked haunted it was this one. It was an enormous old house, with a huge basement. There were strange little many-legged creatures that came out at night from the cracks in the basement bricks, especially when Donnie and Michael played their favorite computer game. The critters responded to the little computer chirping noises. Donnie and Michael always joked that the crickets and roaches were looking for Ms DOS.

Donnie would play the computer game, and Michael would run around scooping up little insects to feed to Mr. T, a huge toad that lived in an aquarium on the upper level with the boys.

Up the stairs was the main living level, where Grandma Kirkie lived in the dining room and living room. There was a big old kitchen and two rickety old staircases to the upper level, where Donnie and Michael and their parents lived.

An even rickitier old staircase went up to the attic. The attic was right out of a ghost story, complete with cobwebs and cracks around the windows that let in weird drafts when you least expected them.

"Yeah," said Donnie. "Say, when you go back to school tomorrow, would you check out a book for me on Morse code?"

"Sure. Maybe the radiator can tell you something besides SOS."

"Yeah."

● ● ●

The next day at lunchtime Michael showed up in his brother's room. "Hi Donnie," he said. "Since school is only two blocks away I got permission to run this book home while everyone else is at recess. I hope you find what you're looking for. I'll check the library again after school. There might be some others."

"Great!" exclaimed Donnie, as he flipped through it. "Look. Right here in the front cover is the complete Morse code. Let me see—*S*. Sure enough. Three dots [usually called "dits" in Morse code]. *O* is three dashes [usually called "dahs" in Morse code]—those must be the long taps—and *S* is another three dots. Yes! The radiator was saying SOS!"

"Someone's in trouble, or something," said Michael. "This is a very old house. I wonder if it's haunted."

"Nah, we don't believe in that stuff, remember?"

"I don't know, but I've got to get back to school or I'll be late and then I'll get in big trouble. Enjoy your book. See you after school."

"Thanks, Michael. You're not bad for a little brother," said Donnie. Michael grinned and disappeared from the doorway.

I don't know how everyone thinks we look like brothers! thought Donnie to himself. *We don't look anything alike. I'm blond with brown eyes and am built!* He grinned down at his broadening shoulders and thickening muscular arms. *Michael is little and skinny and has brown hair. Of course, he does have brown eyes like Dad and me. I always thought that kids looked like a cross between their parents, but not us. We have one mom-clone and one dad-clone.*

It's hard to look exactly *like Mom because that changes sometimes.* Dad had a funny song he would sing sometimes about Mom. Donnie hummed a little bit and then remembered the words:

With your hair so red,
And your eyes so blue,
Freckles on your face,
I know I love you . . .

He giggled out loud. Mom had brown curly hair now. He couldn't imagine her with red hair, but Dad didn't seem to notice. Since she got her new contact lenses, her eyes were more green than blue, and that stuff she put on her face every morning covered up all her freckles. Donnie kind of liked her freckles, since his nose was covered with them too.

Oh well, he thought, *Mom doesn't tell me what to put on my face, so I guess I won't tell her what to put on hers!*

Michael was certainly a Dad-clone, though.

Ever since Michael was born it had been fun to draw glasses and a beard on his baby pictures. He looked just like Dad except short and drooly. He still looked just like Dad but didn't drool as much now!

13

Donnie opened the book to the code page. *Well,* he thought, *I don't believe in ghosts, and there can't really be a person in that radiator. Maybe someone is playing a trick on me. I think I'll play along and try to figure out who it is. I need to compose a message. If it starts tapping again, I'll ask it questions.*

•••• •• *There, that's the first word. Now,* •– •–• • *This is pretty time consuming. I wonder if whoever it is that's sending these messages will talk back to me. I'd better have my paper and pen ready so that I can write it down. It will take me forever to translate it back into English.*

He continued his message. Then he thought, *Maybe if I start tapping first I'll get an answer.* He took his pencil over to the radiator and started tapping. There was no answer. *Maybe I should send SOS. Maybe that will get some attention.*

••• ––– •••

Still no reply, just the usual creaky floorboards as Mother moved around downstairs taking care of Grandma Kirkie.

Poor Mom, thought Donnie. *It must be an awful lot of work to take care of Grandma Kirkie downstairs and me upstairs, and neither one of us able to get up and do anything. But at least I can talk. Grandma Kirkie can't even talk since she had her stroke. She just sits and drools.*

It must be awful for her. Dad said that she was almost blind even before the stroke. I wonder if she can still hear? He shrugged. *I guess I'll finish getting my message ready in case the taps come back. I sure hope they do.*

● ● ●

He was engrossed in his magazine when he first heard them. Tap, tap, tap. Long tap, long tap, long tap. Tap, tap, tap. Quickly he grabbed his pencil and tapped his message into the radiator.

•– •–• •

___ ___ ___ [ARE]

▬ ▬•▬ ▬ ▬ ▬ ▬ •• ▬
__ __ __ [YOU]

••• ▬ ••▬ ▬•▬• ▬•▬
__ __ __ __ __ [STUCK]

•• ▬•
__ __ [IN]

▬ •••• • •▬• • ••▬ ▬••
__ __ __ __ __ __ __ [THERE?]

After a pause the reply started. Donnie was ready with his pencil in hand. He carefully recorded the taps, his brown eyes widening in disbelief as his page filled. "Whatever or whoever it is, is really talking to me," he gasped. "I don't believe it. Wait till Michael gets home!"

••
__ [I]

▬•▬• •▬ ▬• ▬
__ __ __ __ [CAN'T]

▬ •▬ •▬•• ▬•▬
__ __ __ __ [TALK]

▬ ▬ ▬ ▬
__ __ [TO]

•▬ ▬• ▬•▬▬ ▬ ▬ ▬ ▬• • •▬•▬•▬
__ __ __ __ __ __ __ [ANYONE.]

— •••• • —•——
__ __ __ __ [THEY]

—•• ——— —• —
__ __ __ __ [DON'T]

—•— —• ——— •——
__ __ __ __ [KNOW]

•• ——
__ __ [I'M]

•• —•
__ __ [IN]

•••• • •—• •
__ __ __ __ [HERE]

• • •

Donnie was eagerly waiting when Michael came home from school. "Look at this," he said, showing his sheet of dits and dahs and his interpretations. "There really is somebody in there trying to send us a message."

"Wow!" exclaimed Michael. "Who do you think it is?"

"I don't know, but they're stuck in there and are trying to talk. We're the only ones who understand."

"Cool. What do you think it is?"

They both looked at each other.

"I don't know. I don't suppose a real person could be in the radiator."

"No," replied Michael, "it's full of water. Could it be—" his voice dropped to a whisper. "Do you think the house really is haunted? We don't believe in ghosts, remember."

"Yeah," said Donnie. "We decided that on our last camping trip when the ghost stories kept us up all night. Sometimes Satan's angels try to scare people into thinking they are ghosts. But if we're God's kids and ask Him to protect us, Satan can't bother us."

"Well," said Michael, "it's going to be a long two weeks if you aren't going to get any sleep. So since we don't believe in ghosts, let's try to find another explanation."

"Like what?"

"Well, all pipes and radiators rattle and make noises occasionally."

"In Morse code?" said Donnie. "Try again."

"I don't know. Let's not tell Mom and Dad till we figure this out. Maybe you could talk to it some more tomorrow and find out who it is."

"OK. I think I've already got our first clue."

THE FIRST SIGNER OF THE CAST

"All this tapping came around 2:00 in the afternoon, and when I tried to tap back after I figured out the message, I tapped and tapped and nothing happened. The same thing happened this morning."

"Well," said Michael, "maybe whatever it is was only near the radiator during that time. Maybe it does something else during the day."

"Could be," said Donnie. "What should we ask it tomorrow?"

"I don't know. You'll think of something between now and then. Oh, I have the form in my backpack from your teacher about music lessons. It costs $200 a year for the music lesson, but $375 for the instrument."

"Wow! I don't know if Mom and Dad will go for that. With Mom not working so that she can stay home and take care of me and Grandma Kirkie, they might not be able to do that."

"Well, I told Mom about it on the way upstairs. She and Dad will talk about it tonight."

"I really wish I could," said Donnie.

"If you did join the band," said Michael, "what instrument would you play?"

"Well, either trumpet or saxophone. I think instruments made of brass are so cool."

"If I get a vote, I'd choose the saxophone. Trumpets hurt my ears, and I bet you wouldn't be very good at it for a while. At least a saxophone has a little quieter tone."

"Yeah, well it wouldn't be if I was playing it!"

"So," said Michael, "are you going to let me be the first one to write on your cast?"

"Sure, but be careful. My leg still hurts even when it's barely bumped."

"I'll be careful. Let me get my markers."

● ● ●

"What are you doing down there?" asked Donnie.

"Art work," said Michael. "Someday when I'm a rich and fa-mous artist, this cast will be worth a lot of money."

"No, really, what are you drawing?"

"Just mind your own business until I'm done," grinned Michael. "You're pretty nosey for someone who can't catch me this week." Donnie sat back and waited impatiently. Michael stood back and admired his handiwork.

"OK, take a look," he said. There was a picture of a skate-board with a red circle around it and a line through the circle. Michael had written: "No skateboarding zone" and signed his name.

"Thanks," said Donnie. "Now anybody who sees my cast is going to know how I did this."

"That's OK. Nobody's going to see it for two weeks anyhow. And when they do, everyone is going to ask you how you broke your leg."

"If they haven't already laughed me out of the sixth grade," said Donnie.

"They aren't laughing about it at school," Michael replied. "They're really sorry that you got hurt."

"I'll bet."

"Well," said Michael, "I'm going downstairs to see what's for supper. I'm starving." And with a grin he disappeared.

How to Make a Tree

It was Sabbath and Donnie was extra bored. The house was quiet except for the radio that Dad had on downstairs while he cleaned up breakfast. Mom and Michael had gone to Sabbath school. At church time, Mom and Dad would switch, with Dad going to church and Mom coming home to watch Grandma and fix lunch.

Donnie never thought he'd come to the place where he'd miss those sermons by Pastor Peter-the-Boring, but today he'd give just about anything to get to church!

Donnie spent the morning composing his next message to the phantom. It said, "Hi, I'm bored." He found as he went along that he got a little faster translating the letters to code.

He waited impatiently all morning, eyeing the radiator suspiciously. Silence. At lunch time Mom sat him up in a chair and propped his leg up on some pillows so that he could look out the window while he ate.

He eyed the huge oak tree just outside the

window. A stout branch reached over the porch roof and almost to the window. *It sure would be easy to get into the tree,* he thought. *Out the window, onto the roof, grab the branch, and over to the tree. Nothing to it!*

An empty bird's nest two branches up caught his attention. *Not surprising,* thought Donnie. *This time of year whatever birds are left hang around the bird feeder downstairs.*

Sure would be fun to get out and climb down the tree. Wouldn't Mom be surprised to have me knocking at the front door?

He gingerly tried to lift his casted leg. "Ow! Bad idea!" He thought he might try again later when his leg was a little better. He glanced over at the clock on his dresser. One o'clock. *Maybe I should go back to bed,* thought Donnie. *I need to be near the radiator in case the tapping starts. I'll never reach it from here.* "Mom! Mom!" he yelled.

"Just a minute, dear. Dad's not home from church yet, and I have to finish feeding Grandma. I'll be up in a few minutes."

"But Mom, I want to get back in my bed."

"You're going to have to wait," said Mom firmly.

Donnie pounded the arm of his chair in frustration and disgust. Mom was always busy with Grandma Kirkie. What if the tapping started? He'd never be able to answer it. And if he didn't answer, maybe it wouldn't talk to him anymore. What could he do?

He sat and waited, tapping his fingers on the chair. It was 1:30 by the time Mom got upstairs. Gently she helped him back over to his bed.

"What's the matter?" she asked. "Are you hurting? Do you need a pain pill?"

"No, I'm OK. I'm just a little tired."

"OK, sweetie." She fluffed his pillows and kissed him on the forehead. He wrinkled his nose out of habit.

"Thanks," he said.

"You're welcome. Thanks for waiting. I'm going to let Grandma sit up for another half hour or so, and then I'll put her back to bed, too. Call me if you need anything. I'm going down to wash dishes."

"OK, Mom." Donnie lay in bed eyeing the radiator. It was deathly quiet. He picked up his pencil and tapped in his message.

Immediately he heard an answering message.

−•• − − −

___ ___ [DO]

− •••• •

___ ___ ___ [THE]

− •−• • •

___ ___ ___ ___ [TREE]

Donnie paused, then frantically tried to compose an answer. It took him several minutes before he tapped it in:

••

___ [I]

−•−• •− −• −

___ ___ ___ ___ [CAN'T]

− − −•− −

___ ___ [MY]

•−•• • − −•

___ ___ ___ [LEG]

•• •••

___ ___ [IS]

− ••• •−• −−− −•− • −•

___   ___   ___   ___   ___ ___   [BROKEN]

The phantom answered immediately.

Wow! thought Donnie. *The phantom must know the Morse code by heart. I have to look everything up.*

The phantom's answer took two pages of notebook paper, as Donnie busily jotted down each tap. Then the radiator went quiet.

Donnie tried to translate the answer to see what the phantom was saying. His eyes widened in disbelief.

−   ••••   •

___   ___   ___   [THE]

••−• •− −− •• •−•• −•−−

___   ___ ___   ___   ___   ___   [FAMILY]

−   •−•   •   •

___   ___   ___ ___   [TREE]

••

___   [I]

−•−• •− −• −

___   ___   ___ ___   [CAN'T]

•••• • •−•• •−−• •−•−•−

___   ___   ___   ___   ___   [HELP.]

•−−• ••− −

___   ___   ___   [PUT]

•- - - -

___ [1]

•- -

___ ___ [AT]

•-•• • •••- • •-••

___   ___   ___   ___   ___   [LEVEL]

- -•••

___ [7]

Wow! thought Donnie. *It'll take me the rest of the afternoon to figure out all this stuff.* He continued to translate.

"Level 7 is at the outer branches. Fill in your brother and your cousins. Aunts and uncles belong on level 6."

How did the phantom know?

THE PRESENT
FROM JACK STOLL

After decoding the message, Donnie frowned for a few minutes. "OK, I guess I can," he said. Mom had left his sketchbooks and markers right next to the bed where he could reach them. He drew a huge tree and started putting circles all around the edges of the tree, just like the phantom told him to do. He drew himself, a smiley face with ears, and hair, and a cast. He wrote "Donnie" underneath it. Next to that he drew Michael. He drew Michael with very big ears and a pointed nose. "That ought to 'earitate' him," he said with a grin.

He filled in his other cousins around the edge of the tree. *That's not too hard,* he thought. *Now let's fit in everybody's parents and connect the parents to the cousins, like little branches.*

He drew in Dad with his beard and wrote "Bruce," and Mom with her glasses. He put a nurse's cap on her head. *Even though she's not working in a hospital right now, she's doing a lot of nursing between me and Grandma Kirkie,* he thought. *She just doesn't get paid as much.*

It took him quite a while to fill in all his aunts and uncles and write in their names. He looked up and was surprised to see Michael in the doorway. "Wow! Home from church already?"

"Yeah. Church went long, and we stayed for the potluck 'cause Dad had to go to a meeting right after that," said Michael. "Did you miss me? Did the phantom call?"

"It did. Get a load of this."

"Wow! I wish the phantom would help me with *my* home-work."

They both laughed.

● ● ●

The next morning Donnie quickly composed his next mes-sage to the phantom in case the phantom called early. It said "Hi, I drew the tree."

Then he pulled out his family tree and looked at it carefully. "Well, the phantom said I was level seven, so I guess Mom and Dad are level six. I bet I could fill in level five."

He connected all the aunts and uncles to a single branch, level five, and put in Grandpa and Grandma. He made Grandma Jo with a pretty face but no hair, and an IV bottle plugged into her arm. Grandma Jo was getting chemotherapy treatments for cancer. He drew Grandpa Chuck with silver hair with a little black stripe in the middle, and glasses.

"Well, I didn't need anybody's help with that level." The next level would be Grandma Kirkie, downstairs. He drew the branch from Grandma Jo to another branch and filled in Grandma Kirkie. He drew her with a crooked, curly wig, and her left eye shut and half of her mouth hanging down sideways with drool running out of it. He drew her right eye open and then colored over it with his white crayon to give her a teary, filmy look. "Yep, that's how she looks," he said to himself.

This would be an accurate family tree. He laid his markers down and stared out the window. *I guess there should be other branches,* he thought. *I think that Grandma Jo has a brother, and I know he has kids. I wish I'd been paying more attention at the last family reunion.*

● ● ●

The tapping started promptly at 2:00. Donnie was ready with his pencil and tapped in his short message. To his delight the phantom tapped back a very long message. Donnie grinned as he jotted it all down. Later, as he translated it into English with his library book, a slithery feeling started in the pit of his stomach and grew stronger the further he got with the message.

●●●● ●●— —● —

__ __ __ __ [HUNT]

●●—● ——— ●—●

__ __ __ [FOR]

●——● ●—● ● ●●● ● —● —

__ __ __ __ __ __ __ [PRESENT]

●●—● ●—● ——— ——

__ __ __ __ [FROM]

●——— ●— —●—● —●—

__ __ __ __ [JACK]

●●● — ——— ●—●● ●—●●

__ __ __ __ __ [STOLL]

•—•• • •••— • •—••
__ __ __ __ __ [LEVEL]

••••—
__ [4]

•— — — •• —•—•
__ __ __ __ __ [ATTIC]

— •—• ••— —• —•—
__ __ __ __ __ [TRUNK]

••— —• —•• • •—•
__ __ __ __ __ [UNDER]

••• ——— ••— — ••••
__ __ __ __ __ [SOUTH]

•— •• —• —•• ——— •——
__ __ __ __ __ __ [WINDOW]

This was great! A present just for him. And who was Jack Stoll? Maybe Mom would know.

How am I going to find the present, though, he wondered. *I'll have to get Michael to help me.* Just then Mom popped up in the doorway. "How're you doing Donnie?"

"I'm fine." he said. "Ah, do you know who Jack Stoll is— or was?"

"Jack Stoll was Grandma Kirkie's husband," said Mom. "That would make him your great grandpa. He died a long time ago."

"Really?" asked Donnie. "How long ago?"

"Oh, I don't know exactly. Before your dad and I ever met. He died on a bed they made for him in the dining room, and

Grandma Kirkie has slept there ever since. She's never slept in any other room. She says she feels closer to him that way."

"Wow! It's a good thing he didn't die in the bathroom."

"Yes," laughed Mom. "We'd have to build another one for the rest of us, wouldn't we?" They both chuckled for a minute. Then Mom said, "Well, I need to get back down and keep an eye on her. Is there anything I can get for you?"

"Yeah. Can you send Michael up?"

• • •

"Mom said you wanted me to come up right away," Michael said as he raced through the door. "What's up? Did the phantom call?"

"You bet," said Donnie. "And you're not going to believe this message." He showed it to Michael.

"A present. Does the phantom know you have a brother?"

"Don't be silly," snapped Donnie. "It's *my* phantom."

"All right," grumped Michael. "So which way is south?"

"I don't know."

"Wait! I saw an old compass when I was poking around in the tool room. Let me go find it. Maybe it still works!"

He reappeared a few minutes later, triumphantly holding a little broken compass. "Well, the glass on the top is broken, but I think it should still work. Aren't these things magnetic? I mean breaking the glass shouldn't make a difference should it?"

"I don't think so," responded Donnie. They turned the compass slowly until they had the arrow pointing to the letter *N*. "That means that south would be toward the back of the house. Is there a window on the south side of the attic?"

"I don't know," said Michael. "I'll go outside and look." He ran down the stairs. Donnie heard his feet pounding back up.

"Yep, sure thing. There's a window on that side, but there's a shutter over it. That's why we didn't notice any light coming through it when we looked up there on moving day."

"According to this message there's a trunk right below that window. Think you can find it?"

"I don't know," said Michael. "You remember that when we moved in, everybody pushed all that stuff over against one wall in the attic so that we could put our stuff against the other wall. I'll have to crawl over a lot of boxes, and you know there are spiders up there."

"I'd forgotten how sissy you are about spiders."

"I'm not a sissy. I just don't like spiders."

"Well, if you don't go, then neither one of us will know if there really is a present in the trunk or not."

"OK," said Michael. "Can I use your flashlight?"

Donnie hesitated. The big, high powered torch was his pride and joy. He never let anyone touch it. "OK," he said, "just this once since you're on a mission for me."

"Cool!" said Michael, grabbing up the light. "I'll be right back. If you hear me yell, call Mom."

"OK, but I hope you don't need any help, 'cause you know that we aren't really supposed to go up there."

"Yeah, I won't need any help, so don't worry. I'll be back down in a little bit."

Donnie heard the attic door squeak as Michael opened it and climbed the attic stairs. He tried to make a lot of noise in his bedroom so that Mom wouldn't hear Michael. He wished Michael would hurry up. The hands on the clock dragged.

What could be taking him so long? Of course, Donnie thought, *there was no light up there, and there were millions of boxes. What if the phantom doesn't know what it's talking about? What if the box was there a long time ago but isn't there anymore? What if the phantom really is a ghost, and now it's got Michael up in the attic and nobody will ever find him again? What if . . .*

Thump, thump, thump. Donnie heard Michael's feet clattering down the attic stairs. Quickly he dropped a stack of books on the floor and picked them up one by one, dropping one occasionally, hoping that the noise would cover up Michael's clattering down the stairs.

"Are you OK?" Mom shouted up the stairs.

"Yeah, I'm fine," Donnie called back. "Just dropped some books."

"OK."

Donnie grinned. Michael was standing in the doorway, covered with dust and cobwebs, but with a triumphant smile on his face and holding a small, weird-shaped suitcase.

"What is it?" asked Donnie.

"I don't know, but everything else in the trunk was stuff like old dresses, and I didn't figure you'd want those."

"You're right. Let's open it."

They brushed the dust off the case. It wasn't locked. There was a little brass plate next to the catch that said "J. Stoll." Carefully they tried the latch. It was open.

"What if there's like rats or skeletons or something in there?" asked Michael.

"Don't be silly," said Donnie. "Rats couldn't get in there, and well, ah, it's too small for a skeleton."

"Not a small one."

"True, but the only way to know is to look."

The lid creaked as they opened it. Donnie and Michael both caught their breath.

SAXOPHONE LESSONS

"It's beautiful," breathed Donnie. "It's a present for me from Jack Stoll, Grandpa Jack. The J. Stoll on the case means this was his."

"Wow!" said Michael. "How did the phantom know you wanted to learn the saxophone?" He added, "It's a really nice phantom. It didn't give you a trumpet."

• • •

That evening when Dad came home, they showed him the saxophone. "That's great," said Dad. "I'm really glad you found it. Maybe Donnie can take music lessons after all. I think we can afford the lessons if he has an instrument of his own. But you really shouldn't go up in the attic again, young man, understand?"

Michael nodded obediently.

Donnie broke into a grin. "I can take sax lessons, really?"

"Yes, I think so," said Dad. "These two weeks while you're stuck in bed will give you plenty of time to start practicing. I'll try to get you a book at the music store tomorrow so that you can learn the fingering and learn some of the basic notes. It takes a little while of just blowing to get a decent noise out of these things. Grandpa Jack tried to teach me how to play, and for a while all I sounded like was a tortured cat."

"I bet I'll be better than that," said Donnie.

"I bet you won't," laughed Michael.

"Well, either way," said Dad, "the reed on this one is split. I'll pick up some new reeds, too, when I get your book, and then I'll show you how to put this whole thing together. This is a real beauty."

Donnie could hardly sleep that night. *I'm going to start saxophone lessons, tomorrow,* he thought. *I'll teach myself. By the time I go back to school I'll be really good at it.*

MORSE CODE HONOR

"Hey, Donnie, wake up. I've just had the most awesome idea! I'll bet you could get your Morse code honor from talking to the phantom."

"I don't think there is such a thing," replied Donnie dubiously.

"Yeah, there is!" Michael argued. "I saw a guy at the last Pathfinder fair with one. He had a patch with two crossed flags on it. One was white with a black square in it and one was black with a white square. He said it was for learning Morse code. He had an advanced one too. It looked just the same except with a star between the flags. You would have an honor patch, or maybe even two if you got the advanced one, that nobody else in our group would have!"

Donnie chewed on his lip thoughtfully. The idea of having the only honor of that type in the whole Pathfinder group had real appeal. "Do you think it would be hard?" he asked.

Michael whipped out his Adventist Youth

honors book from his bathrobe pocket. "I just happen to have the requirements right here," he said, grinning triumphantly.

"Let me see!" shouted Donnie, grabbing wildly for the book, which was dangling just out of his reach.

"Are you really, really interested?"

"Just give me the book!"

"It's a piece of cake," announced Michael, sitting down carefully on the bed next to Donnie. "There's only one requirement."

"Only one?"

"One," said Michael. "Count it more slowly so that you're sure you're accurate. One."

"OK! OK!" responded Donnie impatiently. "What is it?"

"Send and receive by International Morse Code at the rate of three words per minute using flashlight, whistle, mirror, buzzer, or key. (Five letter words, minimum of 20 words)" read Michael carefully.

"It looks like there's more," observed Donnie.

"Well, there are other choices," explained Michael. "This isn't really the Morse code honor. It's the communications honor. You can get it by sending and receiving Morse code like I just read to you, or you can do it with semaphore code or with wigwag flags."

"Oh," said Donnie. "I guess we'll stick with the Morse code radiator style. It's hard to do wigwag flags through a radiator."

They both laughed.

"This is great!" said Michael, obviously thinking ahead. "We'll go on camp outs, and you and I can send Morse code messages to each other with our flashlights even if we're in separate tents, and no one will be able to figure out what we're saying. It will be our own secret language."

"Sort of like when you were little and talked baby talk, and I could translate and tell people what you were saying but nobody but I could understand you."

"No," said Michael drawing himself up as tall as he could. "Not like that at all. I can translate for you too. And I don't remember ever communicating that way."

"All right. I'm sorry for reminding you that you used to be a baby. How hard do you think it would be to get the advanced honor?"

"It says here that we have to 'send and receive by International Morse Code at the rate of eight words per minute using flashlight . . .' and all the stuff it said for the other one. We could practice sending messages to each other every day. It would help us get faster so that we could get the honors, and you'd be faster translating and talking back to the phantom!" Michael was fairly bursting with excitement.

Donnie frowned. "It's *my* phantom," he said. "*I'm* the one communicating in Morse code. I'm the one getting the honor. What's all this *we* stuff?"

"I'd like to learn Morse code too," said Michael quietly. "I got you the book with the code in it, and I got you the book with the honor requirements in it, and I would really like to do it too."

Donnie looked guiltily at his feet. Michael was right. He had been really helpful, and he had even thought of the honor and gotten all the information early before Donnie had even awakened. He had shared everything, and Donnie felt ashamed. It would be much more fun playing Morse code with a partner. What fun would it be on a Pathfinder camp out, knowing a secret language, but being the only one? It just sounded lonely.

"I'm sorry, Michael," he said, putting his arm around his little brother. "You can learn Morse code with me. We'll practice till we're really good at this."

Michael's face lit up like a Christmas tree. "What shall we use to communicate?"

"I like the whistle idea. Then I can be in my bedroom and you can be here, and we can send messages without leaving our rooms," suggested Michael.

"We only have one whistle, and I'm not sure how long Mom would stand that," said Donnie. "She'll want to throw our whistle out the window!"

"True," mused Michael. "We don't have a buzzer, and she wouldn't like that either. Maybe we should stick to flashlights."

"OK, flashlights will work after dark. In the daytime, let's just tap like the phantom does. We can tap on a book or something so that the phantom doesn't intercept our messages."

"Good idea. We'll need to practice both sending and receiving, and time each other. I'll swipe the timer from the kitchen so that we can set it for 10 minutes and see how many words we can send or receive in that time. Then we can just divide that by 10, and it will tell us our speed per minute."

"Great!" said Donnie. "Can you get it now?

"Oh, no!" shrieked Michael. "I can't! I have to be to school in 10 minutes, and I'm still in my pajamas! Maybe this afternoon!" and he rushed from the room.

Chapter 8

HURTING A CAT?

Donnie started his morning by adding Grandpa Jack to the family tree. He really didn't know what Grandpa Jack looked like, so he drew a handsome man with gray hair and a big brass saxophone. Mom brought up some metal polish and helped him polish and clean the saxophone until it gleamed like gold. Donnie thought he had never seen anything so beautiful in all his life. *And it's mine,* he thought. *It's mine, a present from the phantom and Jack Stoll.*

Dad was as good as his word and came home on his lunch break with a saxophone book and two new reeds. He showed Donnie how to put the reed into the mouthpiece and how to play.

"*You* know how to play this thing?" asked Donnie.

"Sure!" said Dad. "Grandpa Jack taught me. I played in the band when I was in high school."

"Cool!"

"In fact," continued Dad, "This is the very saxophone I played, but it belonged to Grandpa Jack. Mom and Dad were never able to afford to buy me one of my own. New saxophones are very expensive."

"Well," said Donnie, "this one looks brand new since Mom and I cleaned it up. Doesn't it just gleam like gold?"

"It sure does," said Dad. "You've done a beautiful job. I'm going to let you practice now. Don't be discouraged if it sounds kind of weird for a while, because it takes some time to get your mouth set just right."

"I'll be fine," said Donnie. "Thanks for bringing this stuff home for me."

"Sure," said Dad. "Gotta get back to work." And he left.

● ● ●

Donnie spent the next hour trying to get a musical sound out of his instrument. It wailed and it bellowed, and it made some distinctly gastric noises, none of which sounded musical. *Well, Dad warned me about this,* he thought. *I'll just keep trying.* He almost forgot about the phantom, when suddenly he heard tapping coming from the radiator. He leaned over and tapped in his thank you message: "Hi. Thank you. I love it."

The phantom tapped back. Donnie faithfully scribbled down every dit and dah.

●●
___ [I]

━●━ ━● ━━━ ●━━
___ ___ ___ ___ [KNOW]

●●
___ [I]

-.-. .- -.
___ ___ ___ [CAN]

.... . .- .-.
___ ___ ___ ___ [HEAR]

.--- .- -.-. -.-
___ ___ ___ ___ [JACK]

.--. .-.. .- -.-- . -..
___ ___ ___ ___ ___ ___ [PLAYED]

.. -
___ ___ [IT]

-... . - - . -.-
___ ___ ___ ___ ___ ___ [BETTER]

... ..- .-. -. -.. ...
___ ___ ___ ___ ___ ___ [SOUNDS]

.-.. .. -.- .
___ ___ ___ ___ [LIKE]

-.-- --- ..-
___ ___ ___ [YOU]

.- .-. .
___ ___ ___ [ARE]

.... ..- .-. - .. -. --.
___ ___ ___ ___ ___ ___ ___ [HURTING]

45

•—
—— [A]

—•—• •— — •—•—•—
——   —— ——   —— [CAT.]

Hmmm, thought Donnie as he eyed the translated message. *I don't know if I should show this one to Michael or not. He'll laugh at me.* And then he shrugged. *Oh well, he laughs anyway, and he'll laugh when he hears me play this thing. I guess I do need some lessons.*

WHO WAS THE SHORTEST MAN IN THE BIBLE?

"I'm back!" announced Michael, poking his head around the doorway and grinning at Donnie.

"Welcome," said Donnie.

"Here's your equipment," the younger boy said as he placed two glasses on the table in front of Donnie. He poured water into one and left the other one empty. Then he handed Donnie a spoon.

"What are you doing?" queried Donnie. "I'm not thirsty. What's the spoon for?"

Michael tapped the full glass with the spoon. "This is a dit," he said. He tapped the empty glass. It made a different sound. "This is a dah. Here's some paper and a pencil to write down any messages you might receive, and use the glasses and spoon to answer me!" He grinned and ran out of the room.

"Strange boy!" muttered Donnie under his breath, but picked the spoon and stared with interest at the glasses. It was only moments till he heard clinking of a glass and spoon from the next room. Quickly he grabbed his pencil and began to write down the message.

●— ●●●● —— —
___ ___ ___ [WHO]

●— ●— ●●●
___ ___ ___ [WAS]

— ●●●● ●
___ ___ ___ [THE]

●●● ●●●● —— ●—● — ● ●●● —
___ ___ ___ ___ ___ ___ ___ ___ [SHORTEST]

——● ●●— —●——
___ ___ ___ [GUY]

●● —●
___ ___ [IN]

— ●●●● ●
___ ___ ___ [THE]

—●●● ●● —●●● ●—●● ● ●●—●●
___ ___ ___ ___ ___ ___ [BIBLE]?

Donnie grabbed his Morse code key sheet and translated as fast as he could. He was glad that Michael tapped out each word twice. It made him able to double-check his message, and that way he didn't miss little chunks like sometimes happened with the phantom's messages. Quickly he jotted down his answer and began to tap on the water glasses.

━ ━ •• • ━ ━•━• ━•━• •••• •━ • •• ━ •••

___ ___ ___   ___   ___   ___ ___ ___ ___   ___

[ZACCHAEUS]

Donnie leaned back against his pillows and waited for an answer. It took Michael longer to translate his answer, because he hadn't been practicing with the phantom like Donnie had. Soon Donnie heard a giggle from the other room, and the clinking began again.

━• ━ ━ ━

___ ___   [NO]

"What do you mean, 'no'?" yelled Donnie, forgetting he was supposed to be using Morse code. "Zacchaeus is the only guy who was even mentioned as short in the whole Bible!"

"Come on, Donnie! Lighten up! Think riddles," responded Michael.

Donnie stopped to think. They had been laughing and trying to come up with short-guy jokes after Sabbath school the week before he'd broken his leg. He burst into a grin as he remembered one, and began preparing his code to tap back to Michael.

━• • •••• • ━ ━ •• •━ ••••

___ ___ ___   ___ ___ ___ ___ ___   [NEHEMIAH]

"Hey, Michael, let me give you the proper pronunciation," he called, and tapped in:

━•━ ━• • • •••• •• ━ ━• ••••

___ ___ ___ ___   ___   ___ ___ ___   ___   [KNEE-HIGH-

━ ━ •• •━ ••••

___ ___ ___ ___   MIAH]

There was a long pause, and then Michael giggled. "Try

again!" he called.

Donnie thought and then tapped in another guess:

−••• •• •−•• −•• •− −••

— — — — — — [BILDAD]

− •••• •

— — — [THE]

••• •••• ••− •••• •• − •

— — — — — — — [SHUHITE]

Michael laughed after a translating pause. "Let me guess the pronunciation on that!" he called from the other room. Soon his message clinked back:

••• •••• −−− •

— — — —

•••• − •• −−• •••• −

— — — — — — [SHOE-HEIGHT]

"Right," Donnie laughed.

"Oh try again," suggested Michael. "You can find one smaller than him!"

"I can?" asked Donnie. He wrinkled his forehead in thought. Then his face brightened. "What about this?"

•−−• • − • •−•

— — — — — [PETER]

After a pause, Michael clinked back:

•−− •••• −•−−

— — — — [WHY]

•— —• • — • •—•

___ ___ ___ ___ ___ [PETER]

"Yes!" shouted Donnie. "I stumped you! Remember, he slept on a watch!"

"Nice try," Michael called back, but how about someone smaller?"

"Smaller?" asked Donnie, with a sinking feeling. "I give up." The clinking began again from the other bedroom.

•— —•• •— ——

___ ___ ___ ___ [ADAM]

"What?" shrieked Donnie. "That makes no sense!"

"Try pronouncing it this way," called Michael and clinked again.

•— — ••• ——

___ ___ ___ ___ [ATOM]

"You can't get any smaller than that!" said Michael appearing again in the doorway.

"Ooh! Lame!" groaned Donnie.

"No, *you're* lame," laughed Michael, "but you'll be better soon!"

"You're pretty good at this," observed Donnie. "It's a lot more fun doing this together. I'm getting much faster. I'll bet if we did this every day, we'd be fast enough for our honor in no time."

"I'm going for the advanced honor," said Michael.

"Of course, I am too," said Donnie, "but we'll have to work up to it."

RATS!

It was a rainy day, and Donnie was in a foul mood. Life was rotten. He couldn't make a pleasant noise come out of the saxophone, and he was fed up with it. He quit playing, put it away in its case, and lay propped up in bed, and was frowning at the wall when he noticed something that made him even more upset.

A little gray thing ran across the floor, and then another one, and then a brown one. They ran right into his closet.

"Mom, Mom!" he yelled. "Come quick, come quick!"

"Just a minute. I'm giving Grandma her medicine, I'll be right up." Ten minutes later, Mom appeared in the doorway.

"Mom, there's rats or something in here!"

"Yes," said Mom, "mice. There are a lot of them in this old house. Your daddy and I have set several traps downstairs. We killed 36 the first week we were here. I've never seen so many mice."

"Mom, they're horrible; they're gross;

they're in my room. Get them out!" Donnie shuddered.

"I'm afraid I can't get them out right now, Donnie," she said. "I'll ask your daddy to set some traps up here too."

"But I want them out now. What if they come back out again?"

"They aren't going to come up on the bed with you up there," she said. "You're a lot bigger than they are. Mice are scared of giants. Don't worry about it."

"Here," she said. She put a stack of shoes next to his bed. "If they come back out again, you can throw these at them. See how your aim is."

"OK," said Donnie hesitantly. "I hate mice. This is really awful. I hate it here. Why did we have to move here?" he pouted.

"I know," said Mom, "you're having a bad day. Rainy days are hard on broken bones and old lady's joints. I don't think Grandma Kirkie feels very good today either."

"Well, who cares about her, anyway!" growled Donnie.

Mom just smiled. "I have to go back downstairs" she said. And she left.

● ● ●

Donnie frowned at the wall and wondered if the phantom had creaky joints, and he wondered if it would call at the usual time. Donnie composed a message.

"I'm going to complain to it about the mice. Maybe it can do something about them, or maybe scare them away. I wonder if mice are afraid of ghosts." He got out his Morse code book and his pencil, and began composing his message. It said, "Hi. There are mice in my room. I hate them."

He wondered if the phantom could keep up with his tapping, or whether the phantom had to write it down too. *The phantom probably keeps up with it,* thought Donnie, *because it always answers me back right away. I always have to stop and figure everything out. Maybe with a longer message the phan-*

tom will have to pause.

Right at 2:00 o'clock, Donnie started tapping. After a few minutes of tapping, he heard an answering message.

▬ ▬ ▬   ▬•••   •••   •   •▬•   •••▬   •

___   ___   ___ ___ ___   ___   ___   [OBSERVE]

Donnie's forehead furrowed in concentration as he translated the lines. "Observe? I don't want to observe mice. Well, maybe I do. What's the rest of it?"

•▬   •▬•   •

___   ___   ___   [ARE]

▬   ••••   •   ▬•▬ ▬

___   ___   ___   ___   [THEY]

•▬   •▬•••   •▬••

___   ___   ___   [ALL]

▬   ••••   •

___   ___   ___   [THE]

•••   •▬   ▬ ▬   •   ••▬ ▬••

___   ___ ___ ___   ___   [SAME?]

Hmm, thought Donnie, *I did see some brown ones and some gray ones. I wonder what it means.* He began composing his response for the next day.

Is Donnie's Timing Right?

"Today we're going to do speed testing!" Michael stated as he flopped in the chair in Donnie's room. "I spent my lunchtime making a message for you to translate. It has 15 words in it. I'll tap it out to you and time you to see how long it takes you to translate it. To qualify for your honor, you need to translate it in five minutes."

Donnie did some quick mental arithmetic. Fifteen words in five minutes would be 15 divided by five. That would be three words a minute. If he could do it in two minutes, it would be almost fast enough for the advanced honor.

"OK," he said, "I'm ready when you are."

Michael assembled his two water glasses and spoon while Donnie got out his pencil and notepad. "Here goes!" said Michael and began clinking.

  − •••• •

  __ __ __ [THE]

.. -. - . .—. . ... - .. -. —.

__ __ ___ __ __ __ __ __ __ __ __

[INTERESTING]

- •••• •• -• --•

__ __ __ __ __ [THING]

•- -••• --- ••- -

__ __ __ __ __ [ABOUT]

••-• •- -- •• •-•• -•--

__ __ __ __ __ __ [FAMILY]

- •-• • • •••

__ __ __ __ __ [TREES]

•• •••

__ __ [IS]

- •••• •- -

__ __ __ __ [THAT]

- ••• •

__ __ __ [THE]

-••• • ••• -

__ __ __ __ [BEST]

•-- •- •-• -

__ __ __ __ [PART]

•• •••

__ __ [IS]

━•• • •━•• ━━━ •━━
__ __ __ __ __ [BELOW]

━ •••• •
__ __ __ [THE]

━━• •━• ━━━ ••━ ━• ━••
__ __ __ __ __ __ [GROUND]

"Stop the clock! I'm done!" cried Donnie triumphantly.

"Four minutes and 45 seconds!" announced Michael. "Way to go!"

"This is great! Now I need to fix a message for you to time on," said Donnie.

"I'm not ready for timing yet," said Michael. "You've had a lot more practice than I have. I still want to work on it a little more before I try timing myself."

"I guess what we did only counts as receiving at three words a minute," said Donnie thoughtfully. "I still need to prepare and send a message at three words a minute too."

"Yes, that's true," said Michael. "We still have work to do."

UNCLE JOHN'S
GREAT GRAND HAMSTERS

"I'm sorry, honey, I checked with Dad, and we don't have any extra mouse traps. He'll buy some for you today after work, and we'll set some tonight. But for today, I guess I'll pile up these shoes for you again. Those little guys are quick, aren't they?"

"Yeah," said Donnie. "I didn't hit a single one yesterday." He wasn't really sorry though, because they were kind of cute. He had noticed that the gray ones were a little smaller. The brown ones were a little bit bigger, and they seemed to have very inquisitive expressions on their faces, almost like they wanted to talk. As soon as the phantom called, Donnie tapped in his message. It read, "Some brown, some gray."

The phantom tapped back right away:

—••• •—• ——— •—— —•
___   ___   ___   ___   ___   [BROWN]

——— —• • •••
___   ___   ___   ___   [ONES]

```
--•  •-•  •  •-  -
__   __ __ __ __   [GREAT]
```

```
--•  •-•  •-  -•  -••
__   __  __ __   __   [GRAND]
```

```
••••  •-  --  •••  -  •  •-•  •••
__    __  __  __   __ __ __  __   [HAMSTERS]
```

```
---  ••-•
__   __   [OF]
```

```
•---  ---  ••••  -•
__    __   __   __   [JOHN]
```

```
•••  -  ---  •-••  •-••  •••
__   __ __   __    __    __   [STOLLS]
```

```
•   •••  -•-•  •-  •-•  •  -••
__  __   __    __  __   __  __   [ESCAPED]
```

```
••••  •-  --  •••  -  •  •-•
__    __  __  __   __ __  __   [HAMSTER]
```

```
•----  ----•  •••--  --•••
__     __     __      __   [1937]
```

Wow, thought Donnie. He opened up his family tree, and drew a hamster next to John Stoll. John Stoll was level three on the family tree, which meant he must be Grandma Jo's brother. *Wait till Michael gets home and finds out about these mice. I wonder if you can play with them. It would be a shame to kill Uncle John's great grand hamsters! I wonder if they bite?* he mused to himself.

• • •

When Michael came home from school Donnie asked, "Michael, do you know where any empty paper towel rolls are, or any wrapping paper rolls, or anything like that? And do we have any shredded paper anywhere or Styrofoam peanuts, and when you were in the attic did you see any old cages or anything?"

"What are you up to?" asked Michael. "Have you decided to start doing crafts in bed?"

Donnie gave him a withering look. "If I tell you, it's got to be a secret," he said.

"OK", said Michael "I've been pretty good with your other secrets."

Donnie showed him the message from the phantom.

"Wow!" breathed Michael. "I wonder if Uncle John ever got in trouble for that."

"Well, maybe nobody ever knew."

"Except the phantom. The phantom knows everything."

"Yeah," said Donnie. "I think it does."

Michael returned in a few minutes with several empty cardboard rolls, some shredded paper, and an old running wheel out of a hamster cage. "I found these," he said. "I don't see any cages around, but these guys are free anyway. You don't want to catch them."

"I guess not," said Donnie. He asked Michael to lay the stuff around on the floor, and they both sat on the bed and watched expectantly. In a few minutes the little mice were back out. They started dragging the shredded paper across the room until they discovered the cardboard tubes.

What fun they had! They'd run in one end and out the other. For a while they played follow the leader, jogging in and out of the pipes. Then one ran in one end of the tube at the same time as another one ran in the other end. Donnie and Michael chuckled.

There were all kinds of scratching and scuffling as they played tug-of-war inside. Eventually, they saw one little brown tail backing out, and the other mouse pushing him.

"We've made them a playground!" said Michael. "This is great!"

"We've got to keep this a secret," said Donnie. "Mom hates mice as much as I do. We'll have to put away the playground stuff and keep it under the bed, and only put it out when nobody will catch them."

"Right," said Michael.

"I wonder what they eat?" queried Donnie.

"I think they like peanut butter," said Michael. "That's what Dad uses to bait the traps."

"I'll have to ask Mom for some peanut butter-and-jelly sandwiches. Maybe we can tame them and get them to eat out of our hands."

"That would be great," replied Michael. "You don't think Mom will, ahhh, smell a rat, no pun intended, if you're eating peanut butter and jelly? After all, your favorite is cheese and lettuce."

"I don't know. Maybe she'll think my appetite is getting better, and she'll give me one of each."

"Works for me!" said Michael. "I'll save some peanuts from my lunch too, and see if they like those."

THE LOOSE BOARD

Early the next morning, Mom came into Donnie's room with three mouse traps. "Daddy got these for you last night," she said. "I'll help you set them up. We'll see how many mice we can catch in your room today."

Oh no! thought Donnie, *what am I going to do?*

Mom carefully set the mouse traps around the bedroom. She put one outside the closet door, one under the bed, and one over on the far side of the room. Donnie could hardly wait for her to leave so that he could devise a plan to save the mice. How could he protect his friends? Quickly he glanced at the pile of shoes next to his bed.

I hope my aim has been improving over the last couple of days, he thought. He tossed shoes until he was able to spring all three mouse traps. "There, now my babies will be safe." He took out his notebook and started developing his next message for the phantom.

• • •

Two o'clock came, the Phantom called, and Donnie started tapping. His message said, "Hi, hamsters cute. Making friends. You are my best friend, though."

The Phantom replied:

•••• ••− −• −
___ ___ ___ ___ [HUNT]

••• • −•−• •−• • −
___ ___ ___ ___ ___ ___ [SECRET]

− •−• • •− ••• ••− •−• •
___ ___ ___ ___ ___ ___ ___ ___ [TREASURE]

•−•• −−− −−− ••• •
___ ___ ___ ___ ___ [LOOSE]

••−−• •−•• −−− −−− •−•
___ ___ ___ ___ ___ ___ [FLOOR]

−••• −−− •− •−• −••
___ ___ ___ ___ ___ [BOARD]

•• −•
___ ___ [IN]

−•−− −−− ••− •−•
___ ___ ___ ___ [YOUR]

•−• −−− −−− −−
___ ___ ___ ___ [ROOM]

66

●─ ─ ─ ─ ─ ─ ●●●● ─● ●●●

__ __ __ __ __ [JOHNS]

●●● ─ ●●─ ●●─● ●●─●

__ __ __ __ __ [STUFF]

Donnie's spine tingled with excitement. *More secrets! This was great! Now, where was Michael when you needed him?* It seemed like forever until he got home from school. Donnie quietly grinned to himself. *Whoever thought I'd be anxious to see Michael, my own brother. The phantom has ended up making us pretty good friends.*

I bet Michael will be as excited to come home and find out what the phantom said, as I am for him to come and help me find the secret treasure.

Suddenly the door opened, and Mom came in. "I just came to check your mouse traps" she said. "I just emptied the ones downstairs. Oh my, look at these! They're all sprung, and you haven't caught a single mouse."

"I guess the upstairs mice are smarter than the downstairs mice," suggested Donnie, looking at the floor.

"I guess so," said Mom, "and it looks like they ate all the bait."

"Yeah."

"OK," said Mom. "Well, I'll set them again."

"You don't need to," said Donnie. "They aren't really bothering me."

"Well they're bothering *me*," said Mom, and she reset the traps.

Donnie could hardly wait for her to go downstairs so that he could throw his shoes at the traps and spring them before the little mice could come back out again. What if one of them got caught? He'd feel terrible. He quickly threw his shoes and sprung the traps.

Michael would be proud of my aim, he thought. *It's really improving.*

He was glad he had dropped his pillow over the little piece of peanut butter and jelly sandwich on the floor that a couple of his friends had been eating. They scrambled under the bed before Mom saw them. "That was close, you guys," Donnie whispered under the bed. "We'll have to be really careful from now on." He pulled their cardboard tubes back out and lay them on the floor and watched as they romped and played and chased each other through the tubes. "Just be careful to listen for the giant mother," he said. They all glanced up at him and squeaked, and then went on with their play. "I guess you're counting on me to be the lookout."

● ● ●

Three-thirty finally came, and he heard Michael's feet pounding up the stairs. "Michael, you've gotta see this," he said. "Look at the message today," and he showed him the message from the phantom.

"Cool! I guess we'll have to roll up this rug, won't we? I wonder if the phantom knows there's a rug in here now?"

"Well," said Donnie, "I checked this corner over here by the bed, and it's not nailed down, so if we just move the furniture a little bit we should be able to do it."

"Move the furniture? I'm not big enough to move all this stuff by myself, and you have a broken leg. How are we going to move all the furniture?"

"Well," said Donnie, "if we start at that end of the room, we can drag the stuff over toward this end. Then we roll the carpet back just a little and look for the loose board. And if we don't find it, we'll come up to the other side and move the furniture and roll the carpet toward you. We'll be in real trouble if the loose board is under the bed."

"I like the way you say 'we' are going to do all this, like you're going to help too!" said Michael. "You shout orders, while I do the work."

They both laughed.

Michael soon had the carpet back about four feet and started feeling around for a loose board. Sure enough, he found it. As he pried it free, Donnie shrieked, "Let me see! I want to see!"

LILY THE PINK?

"I know you want to see," said Michael, "but I have to pull this stuff out to bring it over there, don't I?"

Michael pulled out a small flat metal box and replaced the floor board.

"I think we should put the carpet back first," he said, "in case Mom comes." He put the carpet back, and moved the desk back over under the window where it had been. "OK, now let's look."

The two conspirators opened the small metal box. Inside there was a skate key, a tiny antique metal car, some old stamps, and a very strange looking green bottle that was sticky and smelled funny.

"This was John Stoll's secret stash when he was a little boy," said Donnie.

"Wow!" said Michael. "I wonder what the bottle was."

"I don't know. It has a label on here, but I can hardly read it because somebody spilled goop all over it. Get your magnifying glass, Michael."

Michael ran to his bedroom, and after a few minutes of rummaging around, came back with the magnifying glass. "It has a name on here, looks like L–y–d–i–a Pink, pink something, I can't read the rest of it. Med–ic– something, something, pound."

"Let me look," said Donnie, grabbing the magnifying glass. He peered at the label for several minutes but couldn't make out what it said.

"Well, let's open it and see what's inside."

"I don't know. It's probably something sticky," said Donnie. "Look what it did to the label." It was very difficult to get the decades-old cork out of the bottle. But when they did, they wished they hadn't.

"What a stink!" said Donnie. "This is gross."

Michael took a whiff. "It smells kind of almost like old cough syrup. It's alcohol, Donnie, there's alcohol in it!"

Donnie sniffed. "Yeah, I think so."

"Well," Michael said, "let's see what pH it is. We have our chemistry papers in the bedroom."

"OK. Go get them."

Michael put a drop on the litmus paper, and they watched it change color. "Yup, that's the right pH for some pretty strong alcohol," said Michael. "Looks like it. I wonder if it burns."

"Do you think we should do that up here?" asked Donnie cautiously.

"Oh, sure," said Michael. He put a drop on a cotton ball. "Let me get my lighter."

"You have a cigarette lighter?"

"I don't smoke. I just found it on the sidewalk," said Michael. "Hang on," and he lit the cotton ball. It flared into a huge flame.

Donnie quickly beat it out with his tennis shoe. "Michael, you could have set the whole house on fire! That was a stupid thing to do!"

"Yup," said Michael, "it's alcohol."

"You're crazy."

"*I'm* crazy? What about whoever put it under the floor boards there? And look at this stuff. I wonder if anybody ever drank it? Gross!"

"I don't know," said Donnie. "I'll ask the phantom."

● ● ●

Donnie eagerly waited for 2:00 o'clock the next day. He started tapping his message in: "Neat stuff. Liked the old stamps and skate key. What is the bottle? Who was Lydia P?"

The phantom answered immediately.

▬●▬● ●●●● ● ▬●▬● ▬●▬

___ ___ ___ ___ ___ [CHECK]

●●▬ ▬● ▬●● ● ●▬●

___ ___ ___ ___ ___ [UNDER]

●●●▬ ●● ▬●▬● ▬ ●▬● ▬▬▬ ●▬●● ●▬

___ ___ ___ ___ ___ ___ ___ ___ [VICTROLA]

●● ▬●

___ ___ [IN]

▬●●● ●▬ ▬●▬● ▬●▬

___ ___ ___ ___ [BACK]

▬●●● ● ▬●● ●▬● ▬▬▬ ▬▬▬ ▬▬

___ ___ ___ ___ ___ ___ ___ [BEDROOM]

●▬●● ●● ●▬●● ▬●▬▬

___ ___ ___ ___ [LILY]

$-$ $\bullet\bullet\bullet\bullet$ $\bullet$
___ ___ ___ [THE]

$\bullet--\bullet$ $\bullet\bullet$ $--\bullet$ $-\bullet-$
___ ___ ___ ___ [PINK]

The message was long. It took almost until Michael came home from school for Donnie to decode it all. As soon as Michael came into the bedroom, Donnie shouted instructions. "Quick, Michael, we have another search! There's a Victrola in the back bedroom, and there's something underneath it that we need."

"What's a Victrola?"

"I don't know. Shall we ask Dad?"

"No. What if it's something we're not supposed to touch?"

"Yeah, let's look it up in the dictionary."

"I'll go find one," said Michael, and off he went.

He came back, grinning, with a large dark green Webster's dictionary. They looked up "Victrola."

"Hmm," said Donnie, "it looks like it's some kind of old fashioned record player. Look for something like that." Michael's triumphant shout rang from the back bedroom. "I found it, you're not going to believe this!"

"I'll believe it. Just bring it in here."

Michael came down the hall, lugging a large box with a huge metal horn on top.

"Wow!" said Donnie. "It looks like those ones on the record label with the dog sticking his nose in the horn listening."

"Yep," said Michael, "I think we have a real antique here."

"Well, the secret was supposed to be under the Victrola."

"Oh, why didn't you say so?" said Michael. He came back a few minutes later with several records. "All of these were in a drawer underneath. Which one do you suppose it is?"

"I don't know," said Donnie. "Something about Lily the

74

Pink, though."

Sure enough, the fourth record down said "Lily the Pink" on the label.

"I wonder how this thing works?"

"I don't know," said Michael. "I don't see any place to plug it in."

"Look," said Donnie, "there's a little handle on the side. I wonder if this is the kind you have to crank?"

They put the record on, lifted the arm, dropped the needle on the record, and started turning the crank. At first all they heard were growling noises.

"Maybe you have to do it faster," offered Michael.

"OK," said Donnie. All of the sudden it sounded like music.

"Faster, faster!" said Michael.

Donnie cranked faster. Soon it sounded like Alvin the chipmunk.

"Not that fast, you dimwit," said Michael.

Donnie slowed down, and eventually they were able to actually hear the words.

> "Oh we sing, we sing, we sing,
>   of Lily the Pink;   ·
> The savior of the human race;
>   for she invented medicinal compound
> That's proved effective;
>   in every case."

"That's great!" said Donnie. "That's the song about Lily the Pink!"

"Who was Lily the Pink?" asked Michael.

"Well, look on the bottle."

Michael peered through the magnifying glass again. "It's Lydia Pinkham's medicinal compound. That's what it said, it just had some letters missing."

Mom came into the room. "I heard music."

"Yeah, look what we found," said Donnie.

"A Victrola?" said Mom. "Play it for me."

They played, and Mom laughed and laughed, and sang along. She said, "This was the theme song of my favorite clown when I was a little girl. His name was Charlie Carolie, and I know all the words to it." She sang along with the record. "I never used to sing the whole song, though, since we only have one Saviour of the human race and *He* didn't sell medicinal compound!"

"Is it true," asked Donnie, "that one of Daddy's grandmas or great grandmas was healed from cancer from drinking this stuff?"

"That's the story," said Mom. "She'd been really sick for a long time, and the doctor said that she had cancer and was going to die. A salesman came to the door and sold them this special medicine. The next day she was all better, and she lived to be a very old lady."

"Wow!" said Donnie. "Do you really believe that stuff?"

"I don't know," said Mom. "There were a lot of medicinal compounds sold back then, and most of them were just flavored alcohol and made people feel good. Some of them even had really harmful things in them like snake venom. I have a women's almanac that has a little article on Lydia Pinkham. Would you like to see a picture of her?"

"Sure!" answered Donnie.

Mom was back soon, with one of her many almanacs. She loves almanacs. Dad said he'd never met anyone who loved facts as much as Mom does. Any facts about anything. Mom has an "enquiring mind." They all teased her about it, but she always won when they played "Trivial Pursuit"! And she knew where to find out about everything.

Donnie scanned down the page, reading about Lydia Pinkham. "Hmm, she invented this stuff in 1876 and said it would cure everything from sterility to kidney distress. That means she lived at the same time as Mrs. White. She gave a lot of the same advice as Mrs. White did about what to eat and getting enough exercise and being clean, but Mrs. White wouldn't have liked her medicinal compound! Oh! Michael! You were right! Listen to this . . ." and he began to read from the almanac. "She had long brewed a concoction of roots and seeds—plus a generous dose of alcohol as 'solvent and preservative'—for her neighbors."

"I knew it was alcohol!" shouted Michael triumphantly.

"Yeah," said Donnie. "This book says it was 18 percent alcohol."

"That's pretty concentrated," said Michael. "No wonder people thought they felt better. It had so much alcohol, they couldn't tell."

"Well," observed Donnie, "her medicinal compound or veg-etable compound as she called it later, made her rich. By the time she died she was making $300,000 a year. That's even a lot of money now. It says the highest amount sold was in 1925, when sales topped out at $3,800,000."

Michael whistled softly. "All that money for this stinky stuff! I wonder if it really worked?"

"Hmm," said Donnie. He thought quietly to himself. "I'll have to ask the phantom."

● ● ●

−● ●−● ●− −● −●● −− ●−
___ ___ ___ ___ ___ ___ ___ [GRANDMA]

−− −−− ●−● ●●● ●
___ ___ ___ ___ ___ [MORSE]

●−●● ● ●−− ● ●−●●
___ ___ ___ ___ ___ [LEVEL]

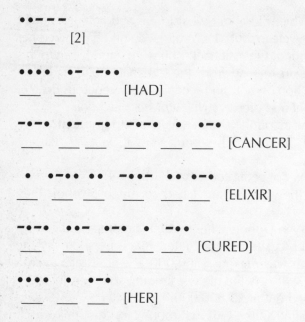

•• — — —
___ [2]

•••• •— —••
___ ___ ___ [HAD]

—•—• •— —• —•—• • •—•
___ ___ ___ ___ ___ ___ [CANCER]

• •—•• •• —••— •• •—•
___ ___ ___ ___ ___ ___ [ELIXIR]

—•—• ••— •—• • —••
___ ___ ___ ___ ___ [CURED]

•••• • •—•
___ ___ ___ [HER]

Michael had been delighted with the message. "Lots of quacks sold healing elixirs back then," he reminded Donnie. "Grandma Morse probably got better because she was almost over whatever they thought it was anyway."

"I wish there was some healing elixir to give to Grandma Jo to cure her cancer," Donnie said sadly. She's just getting sicker and sicker even with the chemotherapy."

"We already know this one is mostly alcohol anyway," Michael pointed out. "Let's do a scientific experiment. I'll pour a few drops of it on your cast and see if anything happens. Who knows? Maybe it really is magic!"

WHERE'S THE MONEY?

Donnie woke up and looked at his cast contemplatively. He peered anxiously at the two discolored spots where Michael poured the "magic" potion. Would it work? Was his leg better? He carefully wiggled a couple of his toes. They felt about the same. Maybe the cast was just a little looser. They still looked pretty bruised.

Michael laughed from the doorway.

Donnie scowled. "How long have you been spying on me?"

"Just a minute. I bet you were hoping that potion had fixed your leg already. If you lived back in those days, you would have lost your whole life's savings buying potions like that. Nothing fixes a broken leg except just waiting for it to heal."

"Why don't you take a long walk off a short pier!" retorted Donnie.

"Can't," said Michael. "Got to go to Sabbath school and church." And he retreated from the doorway.

Donnie reached for his notebook and drew in on the family tree the grandma with the strange looking bottle and a very surprised look on her face. He also wrote a little discovery story about the miracle cure potion. *I'm going to have the best collection of stories in the whole class,* thought Donnie.

● ● ●

After lunch he carefully composed his message to the phantom. He wanted to be prepared when the phantom finally tapped. At 2:00 o'clock, right on schedule, there were the hello taps. Quickly Donnie tapped in his message: "Any hidden money?"

The answering taps clanged loudly through the radiator, echoing throughout the whole house. The phantom sounded really angry.

−● −−−

___ ___ [NO]

●− ●−●●● ●−●●●

___ ___ ___ [ALL]

−− −−− −● ● −●−−

___ ___ ___ ___ ___ [MONEY]

− ●− −●− ● −●

___ ___ ___ ___ ___ [TAKEN]

−●●● −●−−

___ ___ [BY]

●●● − ● ●−●● ●−●● ●−

___ ___ ___ ___ ___ ___ [STELLA]

•—•• • •••— • •—••
__ __ __ __ __ [LEVEL]

•••——
__ [3]

The tapping continued, and Donnie scrambled frantically to get it all down. He missed some, but jotted down as much as he could.

••—• •—•• ——— •—• •• —•• •—
__ __ __ __ __ __ __ [FLORIDA]

—— •• •—•• •—•• •• ——— —• •••
__ __ __ __ __ __ __ __ [MILLIONS]

—• ••— — •••
__ __ __ __ [NUTS]

It took a long time to translate the phantom's message. When Donnie finally finished it, he sat back with a sigh. *I wonder if this stuff is really true?* he thought to himself. *I think I'll ask Mom next time she comes up to check on me.*

• • •

"Mom," he asked, "is there a rich relative named Stella living in Florida?"

Mom stopped to think for a moment. "Yes, I think so. Your dad talks about her once in a while. She's, ah, pretty well off, but sort of eccentric. Last time your daddy called her was Christmastime. He called her to wish her a Merry Christmas. She was busy dying Easter eggs, and wanted to know if we were going to hide eggs too."

Donnie and Mom both laughed. Mom said, "Seriously,

81

though, she and her husband live in Florida, and while they're a little eccentric, they seem to be doing just fine."

"Thanks, Mom."

Donnie filled in Aunt Stella on the family tree. He drew her with slanty, shifty eyes, and she was clutching a big bag of money. He sighed. It would have been much more exciting to find a million dollars behind a panel in his closet or something. Why did all the good stuff have to be in Florida?

WHO'S ON FIRST?

It was a perfect day. The sun was shining invitingly, and there was no school. Michael and Donnie were playing video games on their little hand held video set when they heard a knock at the door. Two of Michael's friends had come over to see if he could come out to play. They played a few video games with Donnie, but soon lost interest.

Donnie detained them a little longer, sharing his markers with them, and offering to let them sign his cast. This they did with a tremendous flourish, drawing silly pictures and writing their names in big scrawling letters. Donnie grinned. Fourth graders just didn't know how to write.

Donnie felt both depressed and relieved as the three boys went out to play. He felt relieved that they had left. He wasn't ready to share the phantom with anyone besides Michael yet. On the other hand, it was a beautiful day, and Donnie felt angry and tired of being left out. He'd been stuck in the house for days with this cast, and he never got to do anything fun anymore.

With a scowl he grabbed his notebook and began composing his message of the day: "Hi. I miss playing outside. I wish I could play baseball again."

• • •

Promptly at 2:00 o'clock the phantom clanged on the radiator. Donnie banged his message in. The phantom completely ignored his complaints. The phantom was in a better mood today, but the message didn't seem to have anything to do with Donnie's problem. Donnie continued translating.

•••• ••− −• −

___ ___ ___ ___ [HUNT]

−• • •−− •••

___ ___ ___ ___ [NEWS]

−•−• •−•• •• •−−• •−−• •• −• −−•

___ ___ ___ ___ ___ ___ ___ ___
[CLIPPING]

−••• −−− −−− −•−

___ ___ ___ ___ [BOOK]

••• • −•−• −−− −• −••

___ ___ ___ ___ ___ ___ [SECOND]

•−•• •− −• −•• •• −• −−•

___ ___ ___ ___ ___ ___ ___ [LANDING]

•−−− •− −•−• −•− •••

___ ___ ___ ___ ___ [JACKS]

-- --- --

— — — [MOM]

•••• •- •—• —•• —••• •- •—•• •—••

— — — — — — — —

[HARDBALL]

Wait, maybe this was about baseball! He continued working. Wow! Where was Michael when you needed him? It seemed like hours until Michael finally came back in, snow covered and laughing.

"Where've you been?" asked Donnie crossly. "I've been waiting for you. The phantom gave me a new hiding place to check, and I can't check it without you."

"Sorry. We were just . . ."

"Yeah, I know what you were doing."

"Where should I look?"

"The message here says hunt for a news clipping in a book, in the shelf on the second landing."

"The second landing? It must be on the back stairs. There are some shelves back there covered by a curtain. Grandma has a bunch of plants all over it. I wonder if it's on one of those shelves."

Michael disappeared and returned triumphantly in a couple of minutes with a big dusty green book. "I hope this is it," he said. "We need a news clipping?"

They leafed through it. It was a big scrapbook. There were hundreds of cards and letters and newspaper clippings all through it.

"How are we going to find the one we want?" asked Donnie.

"I don't know," said Michael. "Let's shake it."

He shook the book vigorously, and out fell a clipping. It was a picture of a lady in a baseball uniform. She was a professional baseball player, and there was an article.

"This is Grandma Stoll," said Donnie.

"Grandma Stoll?"

"Yeah. Grandpa Jack's mother. Listen to this. She was a professional baseball player. Back then they played hardball, but gloves hadn't been invented yet. She must have been a tough lady!"

"Wow!" said Michael. "That's great! We have some really strange people in our family tree, don't we?"

"Yeah. This is going to be wonderful for show and tell."

He carefully drew a stray tree branch from another tree to put Grandma Stoll on where her son, Grandpa Jack, could connect the two trees.

Donnie looked critically at his family tree picture. Almost all the spaces were filled in. He thought carefully and then composed his message for the day. "I've gotta know who's in this first spot on the tree," he said.

● ● ●

Two o'clock came, and he tapped in his message: "Who is on first?"

Quick as a wink, the message came back from the phantom:

●—● ●● ——● ●●●● —

＿＿ ＿＿ ＿＿ ＿＿ ＿＿ [RIGHT]

●—— ●●● ———

＿＿ ＿＿ ＿＿ [WHO]

●● ●●●

＿＿ ＿＿ [IS]

——— —●

＿＿ ＿＿ [ON]

•— — — —
___ [1]

What a wise guy the phantom is!" laughed Donnie. "Who's on first. Give me a break! But look at this."

••• •— — — ••— • •—••
___ ___ ___ ___ ___ ___ [SAMUEL]

— — — — — •—• ••• •
___ ___ ___ ___ ___ [MORSE]

•• •••
___ ___ [IS]

— — — —•
___ ___ [ON]

••—• •• •—• ••• —
___ ___ ___ ___ ___ [FIRST]

As he continued to decode, he got more and more excited. *Samuel Morse? I've heard of Samuel Morse. He invented the telegraph and the Morse code.* Suddenly he stopped, and bit his pencil. *Of course! The phantom does everything in Morse code. The phantom must have been related to Samuel Morse.*

Suddenly, an even more exciting thought struck him. *If Samuel Morse is on first on the family tree, that means Samuel Morse is related to me too!* He continued to decode the message.

● ● ●

When Michael came home from school, Donnie was still decoding the message, and he helped Donnie finish it up. It said:

"Grandma Morse—level 3—married his grandson but was his second wife. Not sure he divorced his first one, since we are not in the Morse family tree."

"Wow," said Michael. "So, we aren't on Mr. Morse's family tree, but it looks like he's on ours."

"We need to ask Dad about this," said Donnie. "I wonder what happened. Family trees should work both ways. Why aren't we on there even if there was a divorce."

● ● ●

As soon as Dad came home, the boys pumped him for information. "It's been a little unclear what really happened," hedged Dad.

"Yes, we know," responded Donnie, "that's why we're asking you to explain it. It's unclear to us too."

"OK," groaned Dad, wishing there were a way to avoid the subject. "Grandma Morse was married to one of Samuel Morse's grandsons."

"Right, that's why her name was Grandma *Morse!*" said Michael, stating the obvious.

"Well," continued Dad, "he had been married before and had a family."

"That happens all the time, though," said Donnie. "Why was that a big deal?"

"It didn't happen all the time back then," said Dad. "Grandma Morse was married to him and had a legal marriage certificate and everything, but she was really afraid that he had never divorced his first wife."

"He had to!" objected Donnie. "It's illegal to be married to two people at the same time!"

"Yes," said Dad, "it is, but that's what she was afraid of. She never had any contact with the Morse family, because she was so worried about it. He died and they had a hard time living without him. When his father died, the Morse family advertised in the papers for any family members to contact them, to be included in the inheritance."

"Did Grandma Morse contact them?" asked Michael. "It sounds like they really needed the money!"

"No," said Dad. "She was so afraid that she'd find out that he was still officially married to his first wife that she never even tried to contact them. So the Morse family never knew about her or her children that were part of their family."

"That's really sad," said Donnie. "Life might have been really different for her if she had just tried. It might have been OK, and they might have been nice to her, and she might have gotten some money to help raise her children."

"Yes," said Dad. "Some people miss a lot of things in life just because they're too scared to try. Now we'll never know what might have happened. Anyway, whether he had an illegal family or not, he *is* part of our family tree, and so is his grandpa, Samuel Morse."

"Yup," said Donnie. "It looks like we should learn Morse code. It's part of our heritage! I'm pretty good at it now."

"Dad's taking me to the library this evening," volunteered Michael. "While I'm there I'll see if there are any good books on Samuel Morse and his family."

"All right! We need to find out all we can about this."

● ● ●

Donnie squirmed in his bed and readjusted his leg on the pillow. Tomorrow was the last day before he went back to school. He would never be home at 2:00 o'clock any more except on the weekends. Would the phantom miss him? Would the phantom think that he had left, never to come back again? There were still so many things Donnie wanted to ask. All his spots on the family tree were filled now, though.

Where was the phantom? Was the phantom part of his family tree? Was the phantom a person from the family tree, or was it just some poor soul caught in the radiator?"

WHO WAS
SAMUEL MORSE?

Michael bounded in with a stack of library books. "I found all sorts of stuff about Samuel Morse and Morse code!" he announced. "He was a really interesting person. It looks like he invented Morse code later on in life after he'd tried a lot of other things. What he really wanted to be was an artist."

"An artist?" asked Donnie.

"Yeah, he liked to paint portraits. He even went to England when he was 19 to learn how to paint them."

"Was he any good?"

"I think so. This book has a picture that he painted of himself. Here," he said, pointing to the page, "what do you think?"

"Looks really good," observed Donnie.

"He was 23 when he did that," said Michael, doing some quick math in his head. "I think this picture is in some museum in Massachusetts now."

"It says here that he tried to paint lots of grand historical events, but nobody would buy his pictures."

"Poor guy. He started the National Academy of Design and was its first president, and was also an art professor for the University of the City of New York. But art wasn't the only thing he was interested in."

"What else?" asked Donnie.

"He liked a good fight, I think," said Michael grinning. "He campaigned against theaters, because he believed the plays made people immoral. He campaigned for Native Americans, because he felt the Indians were treated badly. He also joined groups that picked on foreigners and Roman Catholics."

"Sounds like he made a few enemies," said Donnie. "None of those were very popular causes back then, or now, I guess."

"Well, it says here that he ran for mayor of New York City but lost. Maybe he picked on so many people that there weren't enough left who liked him to vote for him. Still, I'm glad he stuck up for the Native Americans. They really were treated unfairly from what I've read."

"Yes," said Donnie. "We have a great great-grandpa in Mom's family tree who stuck up for the Chippewa and made friends with them during a bad time in Minnesota."

"It was 1844 when he finally got around to inventing the telegraph and the code that he used with it."

"That was the year of the Great Disappointment," remembered Donnie.

"Yeah, for Samuel Morse too, 'cause congress wouldn't buy it," laughed Michael. "Not only that but then all kinds of people came crawling out of the woodwork to sue him saying that they had really invented it or helped with it."

"Poor guy! Instead of being a starving artist, he got to be a starving inventor."

"Not exactly," observed Michael, flipping pages. "Get a load of this," he said, pointing to another picture. "He finally won his court cases and was so famous that he ended up being rich too. He bought this neat place called 'Locust Grove' and built a big mansion there. He ended up starting a famous college called Vassar . . ."

"I've heard of that," interrupted Donnie.

" . . . and giving money to all kinds of things," continued Michael, "like other colleges and churches and seminaries and Bible societies and missions and temperance societies . . . and starving artists."

"Sounds like his life finally turned out the way he wanted."

"Well, I guess nobody's life is ever perfect. He still tried to run for congress, but not enough people voted for him. He spent his summers out at Locust Grove with his kids and grandchildren, and it sounds like they all had a good time."

"I wish I could have known him," said Donnie. "He sounds interesting."

"Well, if this family tree is right, you're part of his big family that he was so proud of, and so am I. I wonder if we inherited any of his talents or abilities. Wouldn't it be neat if one of us turned out to be an inventor or an artist or something?"

"Maybe we just inherited his talent for agreeing with other people," said Donnie laughing.

THE PHANTOM REVEALED

It was five minutes to 2:00. Donnie felt all sad and excited at the same time, with a weird feeling in his stomach. He waited patiently for the tapping to begin. As soon as he heard the first tap, he began his message. It said: "I go back to school tomorrow. I will miss you. What is your name?"

I hope the phantom doesn't mind being interrupted, he thought. He tapped his message in quickly, and waited breathlessly. Would the phantom answer? Would the phantom divulge its name? What if it didn't have a name? What if he had made it angry?

As quickly as always, the phantom replied, and Donnie frantically wrote down the dits and dahs.

•• •-• • -• •

___ ___ ___ ___ ___   [IRENE]

-- --- •-• ••• •

___ ___ ___ ___ ___   [MORSE]

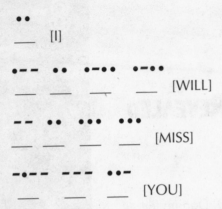

••
— [I]

•—— •• •—•• •—••
— — — — [WILL]

—— •• ••• •••
— — — — [MISS]

—•—— ——— ••—
— — — [YOU]

He sat there trying to decode the message as fast as he could. I–r–e–n–e M–o–r–s–e. Irene Morse? He tapped back in, "Are you in my family tree?"

Quickly there came another tap. It tapped a short message, and then stopped as if in the middle. Donnie waited and waited, and then tapped more, but it was gone. He finished decoding the message, and scowled at his sketch pad.

So the phantom is part of the family tree, and her name is Irene Morse. There's no Irene Morse on this tree, he thought. *Was Irene married to Samuel Morse? No, not according to this book from the library. Who's Irene Morse?*

Just then Mom came into his bedroom. "Hey, Donnie," she said, "are you ready for your big trip out into the big wide world? You've been stuck in this room for almost two weeks."

"Yep," said Donnie, "I'm going to be really glad to get out of here."

"Well," said Mom, "Uncle John is here to visit Grandma Kirkie, and I thought I'd bring you downstairs to visit too."

"Fine."

Mom picked him up and carried him downstairs. She sat him by the big chair in the living room. Grandma Kirkie had been put back to bed. Mom and Dad and Grandpa's uncle John were talking about Grandma Kirkie. Grandma Kirkie was lying in bed, staring at the wall. Suddenly she grabbed her cane, and starting banging on the side rail of the bed.

"Stop that, Grandma," said Mom. Grandma kept right on banging. Donnie just rolled his eyes. Grandma was always banging and making noise, or slobbering, or drooling, or something. Grandma continued to bang with her cane. Suddenly Donnie noticed a rhythm to it. Tap, tap, tap. Bang, bang, bang. Tap, tap, tap. Could it be? It couldn't be! Tap, tap, tap. Bang, bang, bang. Tap, tap, tap.

"S-O-S," said Donnie.

"What?" said Dad.

"S-O-S. Grandma Kirkie is saying S-O-S."

Dad and Mom and Uncle John laughed. "Grandma doesn't understand what she's doing. She's just banging her cane. She does it all the time, and we wish she'd quit it."

"No," said Donnie. "It's Morse code; it's S-O-S." Donnie grabbed his pencil, figured out a message quickly, and then went over, grabbed her cane away from her, and banged this message on her side rail. "I love you."

Grandma turned her head toward the tapping sound. She couldn't see, but she was looking for someone. Then she tapped back a message:

• •

___   [I]

•—•• — — — •••— •

___   ___   ___   ___   [LOVE]

—•— — — — ••—

___   ___   ___   [YOU]

▬•• ▬▬▬ ▬• ▬• •• •

___ ___ ___ ___ ___ ___ [DONNIE]

Donnie wrote it down as fast as he could. "I need a minute to decode this, and I can tell you what she's saying!"

"She's just banging," said Uncle John. "We need to put her in a nursing home. You guys have been here taking care of her long enough."

"But . . . she's giving us a message. She know's what we're saying."

"Could she be trying to communicate with us?" asked Mom. "She sits there every day after lunch, and bangs on the radiator."

"She does?" asked Donnie. Donnie finished translating quickly. "She says I love you, Donnie."

"I don't believe it!" exclaimed Dad. "Tap in some more messages."

"I have something to ask her first," said Donnie. "Maybe we don't need to tap, she isn't deaf, right? Just blind. We could just talk, couldn't we?" He turned to Grandma and asked, "Are you Irene?"

She tapped back:

▬•▬ • •••

___ ___ ___ [YES]

"Ask her how she feels. Do you want to go to a nursing home? Ask her, ask her!" chirped Michael excitedly.

"I learned Morse code when I was a Boy Scout," said Uncle John, "Here, give me that cane." He tapped on the side rail.

Grandma tapped back.

She says, "No, no, no."

Donnie said, "Ask her if she wants to live here with me. Ask her! Ask her!"

John tapped the message into the side rail of the bed. The

message came back quickly. Donnie wrote it down. It said "Yes, I love you, Donnie."

He tapped into the side rail, "I love you too, Irene Morse. Thank you for helping me with my project."

● ● ●

As Donnie finished his report to the class, he closed by saying, "Not only did I find out who the phantom was, but we also found a way to communicate with Grandma Kirkie. We weren't really sure she was in there till she started tapping. Now we know that we can just talk to her, but she had to tap back 'cause she can't talk. I still like to tap messages in for her when I don't want other people listening. It's our secret code!

"I learned a lot about my family tree, too. I guess its kind of like Jesus' family tree in Matthew. There are a lot of different people in there; some we're proud of, some were a little weird, some have great stories behind them, and some are a little embarrassing. All of them helped make up our family and who we are today. I'm really proud to be part of my family!

How to Get Your Communications Honor

Send and receive by International Morse Code at the rate of three words per minute using flashlight, whistle, mirror, buzzer, or key. (Five letter words, minimum of 20 words.)

Advanced Honor

Send and receive by International Morse Code at the rate of eight words per minute using flashlight, whistle, mirror, buzzer, or key. (Five letter words, minimum of 20 words.)

1. Choose your communication method. You may do the long and short components of Morse code many ways. Many flashlights have a little red flash button in addition to the on and off switch, which makes this easier. You may use a whistle to send your messages. You will keep better diplomatic relations with your family if you practice this method outside. Catching the light with a mirror can be very effective. Morse code may also be used with a buzzer or a telegraph key.

2. Find a friend to relay messages to and

who will send messages back to you. Your friend does not have to know Morse code, but must be able to send you the coded messages provided in this appendix and write down your return messages to be checked for accuracy.

3. Practice and build up your speed. When you are ready for testing, have your Pathfinder leader check your sending and receiving speed.

THE INTERNATIONAL MORSE CODE

A	•—	B	—•••	C	—•—•
D	—••	E	•	F	••—•
G	——•	H	••••	I	••
J	•———	K	—•—	L	•—••
M	——	N	—•	O	———
P	•——•	Q	——•—	R	•—•
S	•••	T	—	U	••—
V	•••—	W	•——	X	—••—
Y	—•——	Z	——••		

1	•————	2	••———	3	•••——
4	••••—	5	•••••	6	—••••
7	——•••	8	———••	9	————•
0	—————				

PUNCTUATION AND OTHER SIGNS

Period •—•—•—   Comma ——••——

Question ••——••

TIME YOUR TRANSMISSIONS

Translate the following quotation from Will Rogers and transmit it by Morse code. It contains 18 words. You may just tap the message out as you go, though most people find it easier to translate it on paper first and then transmit it. To transmit three words per minute you must complete translation and transmission in six minutes. Good Luck!

EVEN IF YOU ARE ON THE RIGHT

TRACK YOU WILL GET RUN OVER

IF YOU JUST SIT THERE

Translate and transmit the following message. It contains 15 words. To qualify for the honor, you must finish in five minutes.

A FRIEND IS A PERSON WHO

GOES AROUND SAYING REALLY

NICE THINGS BEHIND YOUR BACK

RECEIVING MORSE CODE MESSAGES

Have a friend transmit the following messages to you. Your friend does not have to understand Morse code to help you with this, but he or she must understand how to make the dits and dahs in the method you agree on. He or she must pause after each letter, with a longer pause after each word, and transmit the message slowly and clearly. You may ask him or her to transmit each word twice, if you wish.

This message has 20 words (punctuation is not included). You must be able to receive and decode this message in 6½ minutes to qualify for the honor. If you can receive and decode it within 2½ minutes, you qualify for the advanced honor. If it takes you longer than six and ½ minutes, don't worry. You'll become faster with practice!

••   •- --   •-- • •-•• •-••

--- -•   -- -•--   •-- •- -•--

•-• • •- -•- ••••• •• -• --•

--- ••- -   - ---

-•-• •••• •-• •• ••• -

•-- •••• ---   •••• •- •••   ••• ---

•-- --- -• -•• •-• --- ••- ••• •-•• -•--

•-• • •- -•-• •••• • -••

--- ••- -   - ---   -- •

How did you do? Try this one. There are 24 words in this message. To qualify for the honor, you must receive and decode it in eight minutes. To qualify for the advanced honor, you must receive and decode it in three minutes.

••• ---   •-•• • - •••   -•- • • •--•

••-• --- -•-• ••- ••• • -••   --- -•

- •••• •   --• --- •- •-••   •• ••-•

-•-- --- ••-   •••• •- ••- •

••• ——— —— • — •••• •• —• ——•

• •—•• ••• • •• —• —— •• —• —••

——• ——— —•• •—— •• •—•• •—••

—•—• •—•• • •— •—• —•—— ——— ••— •—•

—••• •—•• ••— •—• •—• • —••

•••— •• ••• •• ——— —•

—•—— ——— ••— •—•• •—•• ••• • •

•• — —•—— • —

TRANSMITTING MORSE CODE

KEY (Will Rogers Quote):

• •••− • −•   •• ••−•
E   V   E N   I   F

−•−− −−− ••− •− •−• •
Y   O   U   A   R E

−−− −•   − •••• •
O   N   T H   E

•−• •• −−• •••• −
R   I   G   H   T

− •−• •− −•−• −•−
T R   A   C   K

−•−− −−− ••−
Y   O   U

•−− •• •−•• •−••   −−• • −
W   I   L   L   G   E T

—•— ••— •—   ——— •••— • •—•
R   U   N   O   V   E   R

•• ••—•   —•—— ——— ••—
I   F   Y   O   U

•——— ••— ••• —   ••• •• —
J   U   S   T   S   I   T

— •••• • •—• •
T   H   E   R   E

KEY: (15-word message):

•— •••—• •—• •• • —• —••   •• •••
A   F   R   I   E   N   D   I   S

•— •——• • •—• ••• ——— —•
A   P   E   R   S   O   N

•—— •••• ———   ——• ——— • •••
W   H   O   G   O   E   S

•— •—• ——— ••— —• —••
A   R   O   U   N   D

••• •— —•—— •• —• ——•
S   A   Y   I   N   G

•—• • •— •—•• •—•• —•——
R   E   A   L   L   Y

—• •• —•—• •   — •••• •• —• ——• •••
N   I   C   E   T   H   I   N   G   S

-••• • •••• •• -• -••   -•-- --- ••- •-•
 B   E   H   I   N   D   Y   O   U   R

-••• •- -•-• -•-
 B   A   C   K

RECEIVING MORSE CODE MESSAGES

KEY (20-word message):

"I AM WELL ON MY WAY, REACHING OUT TO CHRIST, WHO HAS SO WONDROUSLY REACHED OUT TO ME" (Philippians 3:14, Message).

KEY (24-word message):

"SO LET'S KEEP FOCUSED ON THE GOAL. . . . IF YOU HAVE SOMETHING ELSE IN MIND . . . GOD WILL CLEAR YOUR BLURRED VISION. YOU'LL SEE IT YET!" (Taken from Philippians 3, Message).

The Shadow Creek Ranch Series

by Charles Mills

1. Escape to Shadow Creek Ranch

Joey races through New York City's streets with a deadly secret in his pocket. It's the start of an escape that introduces him to a loving God, a big new family, and life on a Montana ranch.

2. Mystery in the Attic

Something's hidden in the attic. Wendy insists it's a curse. Join her as she faces a seemingly life-threatening mystery that ultimately reveals a wonderful secret about God's power.

3. Secret of Squaw Rock

A group of young guests comes to the ranch, each with a past to escape and a future to discover. Share in the exciting events that bring changes to their troubled lives.

4. Treasure of the Merrilee

Wendy won't talk about what she found in the mountains, and Joey's nowhere to be found! Book 4 takes you into the hearts of two of your favorite characters as you see events change their lives forever.

5. **Whispers in the Wind**

Through the eyes of your friends at the ranch, experience the worst storm in Montana's history and a Power stronger than the fiercest winds, more lasting than the darkest night.

6. **Heart of the Warrior**

The deadly object arrives without warning. Suddenly Joey realizes he's about to face the greatest challenge of his young life. He's answered threats like this before. But never from an Indian.

7. **River of Fear**

A horse expedition brings Joey and Wendy face-to-face with the terrifying results of sin. Wendy goes for help but soon finds herself in more trouble than anyone else.

8. **Danger in the Depths**

Wendy Hanson is missing. Her father and friends from Shadow Creek Ranch frantically begin to search. But every clue draws them closer to the unthinkable!

Each paperback is US$5.95, Cdn$8.05 each. Look for more books in the series coming soon.

The Professor Appleby and Maggie B Series

Charles Mills and Ruth Redding Brand team up to bring you some of the best Bible stories you've ever heard. Wrapped in a plot you're going to love!

An eccentric old professor receives mysterious boxes from his world-traveling sister Maggie B. Boxes bursting with intriguing artifacts and life-changing stories of people who dared to stand for God.

Join Professor Appleby and his young friends in his ancient mansion to listen to Maggie B's stories bring the Bible to life!

1. **Mysterious Stories From the Bible**
Abraham and Sarah, Lot, Joseph, Rahab, Joshua, Hannah and Samuel, and Jesus as a child. 125 pages.

2. **Amazing Stories From the Bible**
Moses and the Exodus, Samson, Esther, and Jesus' miracles. 128 pages.

3. **Love Stories From the Bible**
Adam and Eve, Abraham and Sarah, Isaac and Rebekah, Jacob and Rachel, Ruth and Boaz, David and Abigail, and Jesus' first miracle. 128 pages.

Each book features challenging activities and is US$8.95, Cdn$12.10. Look for more books in the series coming soon.